THE SMELLY BOOK

To Benji Big Boots
The smelliest dog in the world

THE SMELLY BOOK
Babette Cole

RED FOX

Have you ever thought how many

things are really very smelly?

Smelly bags and
smelly bins

contain the most
revolting things.

Smelly cabbage,

smelly fishes,

smelly cheese

for smelly dishes.

Smelly things attract the flies,
especially very old
pork pies.

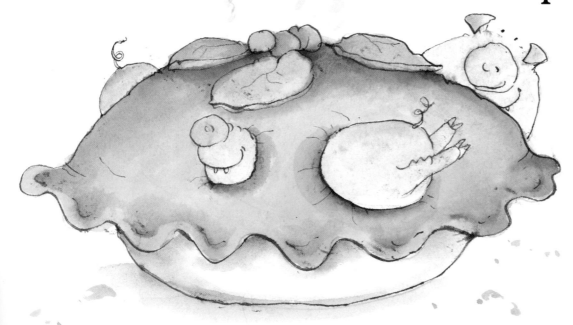

Camels have
a horrid pong,

warthogs can smell
very strong.

I think I would do a bunk

if I saw a smelly skunk!

Smelly pigs

and smelly mice

smelly ferrets are not nice!

Farmers are
a smelly bunch.
They can put you
off your lunch!

Stagnant puddles
smell so
grim…

hold your nose
when you
jump in!

Smelly socks that go quite stiff...

have the most
disgusting
whiff.

My dad's feet smell pretty bad,
sometimes it drives mum
quite mad!

Smelly bones make auntie swoon,

but smelling salts revive her soon!

Our dog likes to roll around

in smelly things left
on the ground

But if I rolled around a drain

I'd never see my friends again!

Smelly babies
wail and bawl.

Smelly tramps don't wash
at all.

Smelly kids play smelly tricks

because some grown ups are such twits!

Teacher said, "I smell a rat.
Who put this thing inside my hat?

...and who threw that rotten egg
at the science master's head?

Whoever did it was quite wrong

to blast the class
with that stink bomb!"

He kept us in 'til after tea.

But never found out...

It was me!

A RED FOX BOOK : 0 09 940961 5

First published in Great Britain by Jonathan Cape Ltd, 1987
Red Fox edition published 2001

5 7 9 10 8 6

Red Fox Books are published by Random House Children's Books,
61-63 Uxbridge Road, London W5 5SA,
a division of The Random House Group Ltd,
in Australia by Random House Australia (Pty) Ltd,
20 Alfred Street, Milsons Point, Sydney, NSW 2061, Australia
in New Zealand by Random House New Zealand Ltd,
18 Poland Road, Glenfield, Auckland 10, New Zealand
and in South Africa by Random House (Pty) Ltd,
Endulini, 5A Jubilee Road, Parktown 2193, South Africa

THE RANDOM HOUSE GROUP Limited Reg No. 954009
www.kidsatrandomhouse.co.uk

A CIP catalogue record for this book is available from the British Library.

Printed in Hong Kong by Midas Printing Ltd

More Red Fox picture books for you to enjoy

ELMER
by David McKee 0099697203

MUMMY LAID AN EGG
by Babette Cole 0099299119

HAIR IN FUNNY PLACES
by Babette Cole 0099266261

THE SILLY BOOK
by Babette Cole 0099417057

TRUE LOVE
by Babette Cole 0099433052

THE RUNAWAY TRAIN
by Benedict Blathwayt 0099385716

DOGGER
by Shirley Hughes 009992790X

WHERE THE WILD THINGS ARE
by Maurice Sendak 0099408392

OLD BEAR
by Jane Hissey 0099265761

MISTER MAGNOLIA
by Quentin Blake 0099400421

ALFIE GETS IN FIRST
by Shirley Hughes 0099855607

OI! GET OFF OUR TRAIN
by John Burningham 009985340X

GORGEOUS!
by Caroline Castle and Sam Childs 0099400766